The Brothers Grimm
Best Children's Stories

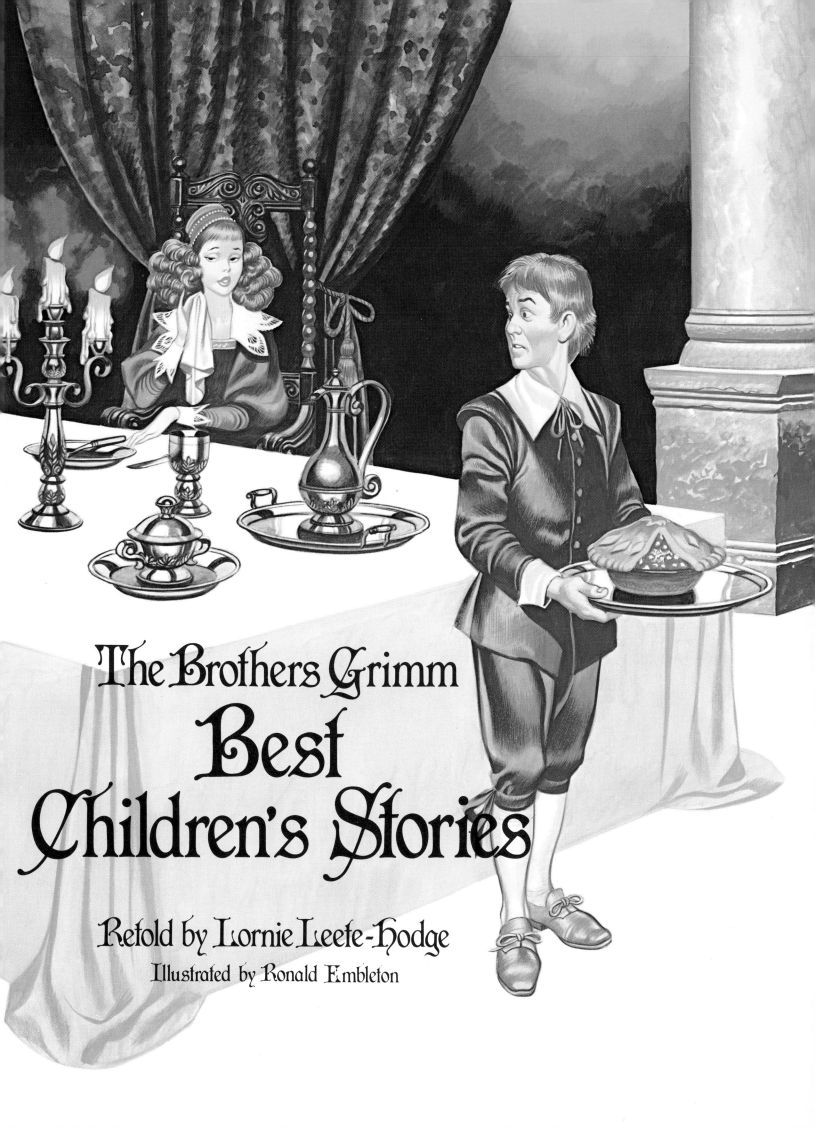

The Brothers Grimm
Best
Children's Stories

Retold by Lornie Leete-Hodge
Illustrated by Ronald Embleton

Originally published in England by Dean & Sons, Ltd.
Published in United States and simultaneously in Canada by Joshua Morris, Inc.
431 Post Road East
Westport, CT 06880
Copyright © The Hamlyn Publishing Group, Ltd. 1983
All Rights Reserved

ISBN 0-887-05059-X

Made and printed in Great Britain by
Purnell and Sons (Book Production) Ltd.,
Member of the BPCC Group, Paulton, Bristol

Contents

Snow White and the Seven Dwarfs

Long years ago in a far away land, a Queen sat by her window sewing. It was the depth of winter and the garden was white with snow. Nothing stirred and all was still. Suddenly, a raven flew down to the grass, his feathers black and shiny as night against the snow. As she watched, he pecked at the ground, and the Queen, taking her eyes from her work, pricked her finger. A bright crimson drop of blood fell. The Queen made a wish.

"I wish that I might have a daughter whose skin is as white as snow, whose lips are as red as blood, and whose hair is as black as ebony."

The raven flew off high into the sky and the Queen looked after him until he was just a speck in the distance.

Time passed and the Queen's wish came true. A daughter was born to her, a lovely child with hair as black as ebony, lips as red as blood and skin as white as driven snow. The Queen was delighted and called her Snow White.

Sadly, soon after, the Queen died and the King married again. The new Queen was beautiful and proud. She was also an enchantress with strange powers and some were afraid of her. Snow White grew into a beautiful girl, her dark hair, crimson lips and white skin the envy of all.

Now the Queen was vain, and loved to gaze at her reflection in the mirror that hung on the wall. This was a magic mirror, and the Queen would ask it a question every day:

"Mirror, mirror on the wall
Who is the fairest of us all?"

And she would smile and preen and arch her head. For the mirror would always reply:

"You, O Queen, are fairest of all."

The Queen would gaze and gaze at her face, reflected in the glass. She looked this way and that, the mirror was right, there was no one more beautiful in all the land.

As the years passed, and as she grew up Snow White grew more beautiful. When she was seventeen she was more beautiful than the Queen herself.

One morning the Queen looked in her mirror and said, believing she knew the answer:

"Mirror, mirror on the wall
Who is the fairest of us all?"

And, to her horror, the mirror replied:

"Thou art fair, O Queen, 'tis true,
But Snow White is fairer than you."

The Queen stamped her foot in rage. The mirror must have lied! She asked it again, but, in her heart, she already knew the truth. Snow White *was* more beautiful than she. Oh, it was more than she could bear! She must get rid of the girl. She, the Queen, was the most beautiful in all the land. No one, but no one should take her place.

"Tell the huntsman to come here at once," she ordered.

When he came, a tall man in his green clothes, he bowed low before her.

"You must take Snow White deep into the forest," ordered the Queen. "There, you must kill her and bring her heart to me."

The huntsman trembled but he dared not disobey the Queen. So he took Snow White with him, deep, deep into the dark forest and took out his knife.

"Oh please don't kill me," begged Snow White. "I promise you I will never come back. Let me run into the forest. Don't kill me, dear Huntsman."

The huntsman was a kind man with children of his own. So he had pity on Snow White and put away his knife.

"Run away, little Snow White," he said. "Run as fast as you can, before I change my mind." And he turned away so that he did not see her go. He thought the wild beasts would devour her. In a thicket, he found a wild boar, which he killed, then he took its heart back to the Queen and told her it was the heart of Snow White. "Oh is it really so?" The Queen danced with joy, and put the heart in a special box so that she could look at it. Her rival was no more! She was the fairest in all the land! She rewarded the huntsman with a golden horn, for he had served her well.

Meanwhile, in the forest Snow White wandered all day. She took first one path then another, sometimes she would feel the great branches of the trees against her, but they did not hurt her. Now and

then, she met a wild animal and stood still, but no harm came to her. At last, worn out with her walking, Snow White came to a little clearing at the edge of the forest. A tiny house, with a little blue door and bright red roof met her eyes. She knocked on the door, lifting the brass knocker and rapping sharply. There was no answer. Snow White tried the latch and the door opened. She went inside.

"Is anyone there?" she called out. "Hellooo!" she called more loudly. But no one answered.

Snow White found herself in a pleasant room, with a big fireplace filled with logs, and shiny pots on the mantelshelf. There were seven little chairs near the fire, with seven little pairs of slippers, one pair beside each chair. And in the corner was a long table, with seven small chairs, each one in its special place. The table was covered with a large white cloth, smooth and fresh, and there were seven places laid for a meal. In front of each place was a tiny knife and fork, with shiny spoon at the side. There were tiny plates, each with a small brown loaf on it, and little glasses, with a bright red drop of wine, were placed in front. The bigger plates were filled with vegetables and a sort of porridge that looked delicious. Snow White was very hungry. She looked at the food.

9

"Surely no one will mind if I take just a *tiny* piece from each plate," she said to herself. And she took the smallest morsel from each loaf and plate. Then she had a sip of the wine from every glass.

By now, she was feeling very tired. The cottage was warm and inviting, and she went up the twisty staircase to the next floor. She found a large room, spotlessly clean, with a row of seven little beds pushed against the wall. Each bed had its own little counterpane, stretched smooth and straight without a single wrinkle.

"I think I'll just lie down for a moment," said Snow White.

She tried the first bed. That was too short. She tried the next which was too narrow. The next was too wide, the next too long. And so it went on, until she came to the last bed. She lay down and found it the softest, most comfortable bed she had ever slept on. In a twinkling, she was fast asleep.

10

When it was dark the owners of the little cottage came home. They were seven little dwarfs who worked in the mines, deep down in the far mountain. All day they toiled for gold and came home to their cottage every night. Tidily, they put their picks and shovels in the corner and hung up their little caps. No sooner had they lit their tiny, candle lights, than they saw that something had happened! Their home looked *different*! The house was not as they had left it.

The first dwarf said, looking round, "Who has been sitting on *my* chair?"

The second asked, "Who has been eating *my* bread?"

The third wanted to know, "Who has been eating *my* potatoes?"

The fourth yelled, "Who has been using *my* fork?"

The fifth asked sadly, "Who has moved *my* spoon?"

The sixth said, "Who has been cutting with *my* knife?"

And the seventh wailed, "Who has drunk *all* my wine?"

The dwarfs looked all around, peering in every nook and corner.

The cottage looked the same, except that their supper had been disturbed. It was all very worrying.

"Let's go upstairs," suggested the eldest dwarf. And so one by one, each holding his tiny light high so that he could see the way, the dwarfs tiptoed up the staircase.

The first dwarf peeped into the bedroom. "Who has been sleeping in my bed?" he whispered. The others crowded round him. They soon saw that all their beds had been slept in.

"Look!" said the seventh dwarf in a scary voice. "There is someone in my bed!"

The rest held their breath. They looked at Snow White lying fast asleep in the bed and were so enchanted with her, they did not wake her. So the seventh dwarf had no bed to sleep on. His brothers took it in turns to let him have their beds for an hour at a time. And so the night passed.

In the morning Snow White was frightened when she saw the seven little dwarfs looking at her. But they smiled and were so kind to her that she forgot to be afraid, and she told them her story. "Who are you? And how did you find our cottage?" They all wanted to know *everything*.

"My name is Snow White," she told them, "and I found the cottage just by wandering in the forest. I had walked all day and seen no one. Please let me stay. I will cook and clean for you."

So it was agreed. Snow White stayed with the dwarfs. Every morning they set off for the gold mines, and she cooked their suppers, cleaned the house, and made everything ready for their return.

"Take care," they warned her. "If your stepmother finds out you are here, she will come. Don't let anyone into the house."

For a while all was well, then the Queen decided to ask her mirror once more if she was the fairest in the land. To her horror the mirror replied:

"You are fair, my Queen 'tis true
But Snow White is fairer far than you.
Snow White dwells with seven little men
And is as fair as you and as fair again."

When the Queen heard this, she could not believe her ears. She asked the mirror twice more, but she knew it spoke the truth. She must make her plans.

Next morning, dressed as an old pedlar, she came to the dwarfs' cottage in the woods, using her magic powers to find Snow White.

"Laces and ribbons for sale," she called out. She held up a bunch of red and blue ribbons. "Come and see," she said in a soft wheedling voice.

Snow White thought the old woman looked so harmless she could not harm her, and opened the door to buy some ribbons.

"Goodness me, child," said the old woman, "your laces are too slack. Come, let me fix them for you." And she laced Snow White's dress so quickly and so tightly that the poor girl fell down as though she were dead. All her breath had gone. And the Queen sped away to her palace.

When the dwarfs came home and found Snow White, pale and white lying on the floor, not breathing, they were very worried. Tenderly they lifted her on to the table, and then saw the tight lacing. One of them took up a knife and cut the lace away. Soon, her colour came back and she breathed easily.

"Take care, Snow White," the dwarfs said, "we warned you not to let anyone into the house when we were out."

And Snow White promised to be careful in future.

When the Queen reached the palace she took off her old clothes and ran to the magic mirror to ask if she was *now* the fairest in the land. But yet again it replied:

"Snow White dwells with seven little men
And is as fair as you and as fair again."

The Queen paled with anger. She knew that the dwarfs must have saved Snow White. She must make more plans. Using her magic spells she made a comb. This was no ordinary comb, but a magic comb filled with poison, one touch and the wearer would die.

When she came to the cottage, Snow White remembered the dwarfs' warning and would not open the door. This old woman looked different, but she had promised the dwarfs.

"Come Lovey," coaxed the old woman, "this beautiful comb would look pretty in your hair. See how it would shine against the darkness of your curls." And she held it out for Snow White to see. She twisted it one way and another so that sunlight caught the jewels that sparkled on the comb. Snow White clapped her hands. It was enchanting! She took two coins from the box where the dwarfs kept their money, and handed it to the old woman through the window.

"Turn round and I will put it in for you," said the old woman, jabbing the comb into Snow White's hair. In a second she fell down, unconscious. The Queen hurried back to the palace once more rubbing her hands with delight. This time she was the fairest in the land, no doubt about it!

It was not long before the dwarfs came home and found poor Snow White. They suspected the wicked Queen and soon found the comb in her hair. As soon as they pulled it out, before it had had time to work all its magic, Snow White stirred and soon she was well again and told them what had happened.

"Never let anyone into the house," they warned. "Take care."

The Queen did not hurry to her mirror this time. She was sure that Snow White was dead. But at last she wanted to hear the mirror reassure her, and she asked it:

"Mirror, mirror on the wall
Who is the fairest of us all?"
And the magic mirror said:
"Snow White dwells with seven little men
And is as fair as you and as fair again."

The Queen knew it did not lie. She went to her room and opened the door of her most secret cupboard. She took out a book of spells and pots and jars. She would make a magic apple! That would not fail. All night she worked, the mixture had to be just right. She stirred this, and she pounded that, and at last everything was ready. She had a basket of apples, these would tempt anyone, and one very special apple, red and shining, lay on top.

Next day the dwarfs set off as usual for the mine. "Take special care," they warned Snow White. "Remember, don't open the door to anyone. Not anyone."

"I promise," said Snow White and waved to them from the window. The door was firmly bolted and barred. She had learnt her lesson. She sang as she swept and dusted and prepared a special meal for the dwarfs who had become her friends. She polished all the plates and pewter mugs that stood along the mantelpiece, shook the coloured mats that covered the floor, and soon the whole cottage was as spick and span as anyone could wish. Then there was a knock at the door.

"Who is there?" asked Snow White. "I may not open the door."

"There's no harm in looking, is there?" asked a soft voice.

Snow White leant out of the window. On the doorstep stood a smiling lady, one she had not seen before. In her hand she held a basket of the rosiest, shiniest apples you have ever seen. She lifted one up and offered it to Snow White.

"Here you are," she said, "a present for you."

Snow White hesitated. The apple looked lovely. Surely it would be all right.

"What, are you afraid you will be poisoned?" laughed the lady. "See, I will bite this half and you can bite the other." And she took a huge bite out of one side of the apple.

It was too much. Snow White leaned out and took the apple. It was firm and red and shiny, just waiting to be eaten! She dug her small, white teeth into the crunchy apple. Scarely had a piece touched her lips than she fell down as if dead!

"Ha! Ha! Ha! That's done for you at last," cackled the Queen. Her eyes sparkled. "This time even the dwarfs will not bring you back to life."

The mirror answered truthfully once more to her question. "Thou, O Queen art the fairest of us all." But she asked it twice more to make really sure.

When the dwarfs came home that evening they found poor Snow White lying on the ground. Nothing they could do revived her. For three days and nights they sat and watched her and wept, but she did not stir. So they made a special box to put her in with a glass lid so that they could look at her beautiful face. For her cheeks were still red, her hair dark and shining, and they could not bear to hide her in the ground. They placed the box on the mountain top, guarding it always, and, in tiny gold letters, put her name SNOW WHITE so that all would know her.

Time passed and Snow White lay as if sleeping on the mountain top. The birds came and watched over her—first a raven, its feathers as black as soot. Then an owl who flew low over her at night, and in the morning flew away, when a pure white dove hovered above her.

One day, a handsome Prince came to the wood and saw the dwarfs' house. He watched the dwarfs and saw that one of them went to the mountain top. He followed, and saw Snow White lying in her box looking as beautiful as anyone could be.

"Give her to me," he said to the dwarf, "I must look at her always. I shall die if I don't." And the poor Prince offered the dwarf all the gold in his kingdom.

"We would never part with her," said the dwarf, "not for gold or silver, or anything."

"I cannot live without her," cried the Prince, and he wept. He begged the dwarfs to let him take Snow White away. They felt sorry for him, and agreed, with a heavy heart. The Prince's servants lifted the box and as they did so, the piece of apple that Snow White had eaten fell from her lips, and she awoke, alive and well!

"Where am I?" she said, looking around her.

The dwarfs clapped their hands in delight. "Snow White, oh Snow White, you are well," they cried, dancing and laughing.

The Prince lost no time in declaring his love for her, and Snow White happily agreed to marry him. They set off for his kingdom and the dwarfs polished their shoes, pressed their best suits and packed up ready to go to the great wedding feast. Everyone for miles around was invited. Among the guests was the Queen. She dressed herself carefully for the wedding, she must look her best. Never had she looked so magnificent. On her way to her coach, she paused, looked in her magic mirror and asked:

"Mirror, mirror on the wall
Who is the fairest of us all?"
Back came the reply:
"You are fair, my Queen, 'tis true
But the Prince's bride is more fair than you."
She could not believe her ears. Snow White alive! For she knew that only Snow White was more beautiful in the whole world. She asked the magic mirror again and again. Always the same answer.

In her rage, the Queen took the magic mirror and smashed it to the ground into a hundred pieces. With it also went the Queen's power and beauty. She raged and screamed and stormed and stamped her feet, until she fell down dead with fury among the pieces of her mirror! Never again would it tell anyone who was the fairest in the land.

As for Snow White, she married the handsome Prince and lived happily ever after, with the dwarfs never far away.

The Four Musicians of Bremen

There was once a man who had a donkey. Now this donkey had served him faithfully and well for many years, carrying his flour to the mill. But the donkey was getting old, he puffed and panted when the load was heavy, and his poor old legs would not move fast, however much his master urged him on with a stick.

"How much do you think I shall get for the donkey's skin?" the man asked his wife one day.

"Good price, I daresay," she replied.

The donkey, who had been waiting with the cart, heard all he said, and knew his master wanted to get rid of him. So, as soon as he was free of the shafts, he set off along the road to Bremen.

"I have a fine voice," he brayed. "I will be the town musician."

When he was well on the way, he saw a large dog lying by the side of the road. He was old and tired and yawned as the donkey came up to him.

"Hello, old dog," said the donkey. "What are you doing?"

"Hello, old donkey," replied the dog. "I am having a rest before I go on my way. My master wants to get rid of me. I cannot hunt as I used to, my legs won't let me run so swiftly. So I am off to seek my fortune somewhere."

"Why not join me?" said the donkey. "I have a fine voice and am off to Bremen to be the town's musician. Come along, too, I am sure you have a good voice."

"Well, my voice is as strong as ever," said the dog. "Why not?"

And he fell in step with the donkey. They did not hurry, and had all the time in the world.

Soon they saw a fine cat sitting on a gateway in the sun. He looked very miserable, as if the rain were falling.

"Hey, there!" called the donkey who always spoke first. "Why so glum? It's a lovely day."

"Maybe so," answered the cat, "but I am getting old. I cannot chase the mice as I once could, and my mistress is going to drown me in the well. I am running away and having a rest on this gate. I don't know where to go. Oh, what shall I do?" And the cat lifted his voice in a yowl.

"Do?" said the dog, "Why, join with us of course. You have a fine voice, even if you are old. We are off to Bremen to be the town's musicians. Two or three, what will it matter? Come along with us, and welcome."

So the cat jumped off the gate and fell in beside the donkey. He was still a bit shy of the dog in spite of what he said. And, if he got tired, he could always ride on the donkey's back.

The three friends went on their way. The road was long and dusty and, round a bend, they came across a farm cock sitting on a barn door crowing loudly.

"Goodness me," said the donkey, "what a noise! Why do you do that?" And he shook his long ears to clear the sound.

"I'm telling everyone it will be a fine day tomorrow. Fine for some that is, not for me. We have some visitors coming, and the cook wants to make soup with my bones. So why I am crowing, I don't know. What shall I do?"

"Oh that's easy," said the cat. "Come with us. We are off to Bremen to be the town's musicians. With the donkey's bray, the dog's bark, my miaow and your crow, that should be just right. What do you say?"

"I've nothing to lose," said the cock. He gave a last crow, and jumped off the barn door and joined the others.

Bremen was still a long way off when night fell. The donkey and dog lay down near a tree, but the cat and cock climbed up into the branches where it was safer for them. The cock flew to the top and called down excitedly.

"There is a small house, just up ahead. We'd be warm there. I can see a light. Come on, let's go."

So the four friends set off towards the light. They could see the lights shining out into the road from a small house. They peered in the window, and what a sight met their eyes! A band of robbers was seated round the table, which was spread with good food. All around them was gold and silver and jewels they had stolen, and a warm fire glowed in the fireplace. It was very inviting.

"Oh, if only we were inside," moaned the cat who was always depressing.

"Let's think of a plan," said the donkey. "We must find a way of getting them out. Then we can go in." So they went back into the woods and talked and talked. At last, they had an idea. They went quietly back to the house. The robbers were still eating and drinking and making merry.

"Come on, now," said the donkey.

As he was the biggest, the donkey stood with his front hoofs on the windowsill. The dog who was the next in size, jumped on to the donkey's back. The cat climbed up on to the dog's back and his fur rippled as he dug his claws in.

"Steady," the dog muttered, "those claws are sharp!"

The cock flew up and perched on the cat's back. When they were all ready, the donkey brayed, the dog barked, the cat miaowed and the cock crowed as he had never done before. You have never heard such a horrible noise in all your life!

The robbers were terrified and ran out of the house, away into the forest. And the joyful animals ran into the house and fell on the feast. When they had eaten and drunk all they could manage, they settled down for the night. They put out the light and found somewhere to sleep. The donkey stretched himself on some straw in the yard. The dog lay on a mat behind the door. The cat curled up on the hearth. The fire was nearly out, but it was still warm. And the cock flew up on to a high beam. He felt safer there.

Meanwhile the robbers were in the forest. All was quiet. "Let's go back to that house," said one. "It was the best hide-out we have ever had, let's go back there. That was only a noise we heard. Come on."

So they crept back, one by one. The boldest of them went into the house. It looked just as it always did. The dying fire gave out a little light, so he stooped down to pick up what he thought was a spark to bring the fire to life. He held a match to the cat's eyes, which shone in the dark. Leaping up with a yowl, the cat scratched his face and hands.

The robber ran to the door, but the dog who had heard him leapt up and bit his leg! Out in the yard the robber fell over the donkey who kicked him hard, and, as if this were not enough, the cock, roused from his sleep, crowed and crowed with all his might.

The terrified robber ran back to the others, bleeding, sore and scared.

"The place is full of monsters," he gasped. "Something spat at me in the kitchen, something else bit me. I have been kicked and there is a terrible judge in the roof who calls my name. I was lucky to get out alive!"

So the robbers went on their way, leaving the house to the four musicians. They decided the house was just right. They had no need to travel on to Bremen to be the town musicians. They could stay there, and make all the music they wanted. And that is what they did. So if ever you find a lonely house with strange music coming from it, it *may* be the four musicians of Bremen practising!

The Elves and the Shoemaker

Once there was a poor shoemaker. He worked hard, day and night but he had little money. Times were hard, and at last he and his wife had only one loaf of bread in the cupboard.

"This is the last loaf," the woman told her husband.

"And this is the last piece of leather," he replied. "It is only enough for one pair of shoes. I don't know what to do."

So the wife cut some of the bread for her husband. He sat at his bench and, taking up his knife, cut out the shoes, ready to sew next day. With a heavy heart the couple went to bed.

Imagine their surprise next morning when they looked at the work bench! The leather had gone. In its place was a fine pair of shoes. The shoemaker picked them up and looked at them very carefully. They were perfect. The uppers just met the soles, the stitching was fine and strong. He could not make a better pair himself. He scratched his head. It was all very odd.

"Are those shoes for sale?" asked a voice. The shoemaker jumped. He had not heard the man come into the shop.

"Of course," he said holding them out.

"I'll try them on," said the man and he found they fitted perfectly.

He paid a good price for the shoes and the shoemaker was able to buy more leather and food. That night he cut out two pairs of shoes and left them on his work bench to sew next day.

Once again his work had been done for him. Two perfect pairs of shoes lay on the bench. These sold as quickly as the first pair, and soon the shoemaker had enough money to buy leather for four pairs of shoes. He cut them out and, once again, they were finished next day.

So it went on for weeks. The shoemaker grew rich and famous, for people came for miles to buy his shoes.

One night, near Christmas, he said to his wife, "Let's wait up and see who it is that is making our shoes for us."

So they left the candle burning and hid. They had not long to wait. Two tiny, ragged elves appeared and sat down at the bench. They began to stitch, sew and hammer, working so quickly that the shoemaker's eyes danced as he watched them. As soon as all the shoes were made, they scampered off as fast as they had come.

"Well I never!" said his wife. "Those poor little mites. There must be some way of saying thank you to them for all their work."

"Blest if I know what to say," said the shoemaker scratching his head. He had never seen the like.

"I know. I'll make them each a little coat and trousers, with a shirt and socks, and you, why you can make them a pair of shoes."

So they worked hard all the day and, in the evening, they put the little coats, trousers, shirts, socks and shoes on the work bench.

Then they hid to see what would happen.

Just as the clock struck midnight, the little men appeared. At first they looked all round for the shoes to sew. Then they saw the clothes laid out for them. In a trice they put them on and began dancing round and round. They began to sing, a happy song:

"Now we're dressed all fine and neat,
We do not cobble for others' feet."

And they skipped and danced all the way down the street. The shoemaker never saw them again. But the good luck they had brought remained, and the shoemaker and his wife prospered. They never forgot the little elves who had helped them. Maybe they are still dancing now?

The Frog Prince

One sunny day a beautiful Princess was playing in the woods with her favourite toy. It was a lovely, golden, shiny ball that glistened and sparkled in the sunlight. Her father, the King, had given it to her on her last birthday. She played with it every day, throwing it into the air and catching it, rolling it along the ground and running after it. No one had ever had such fun with a plaything in all the world.

The Princess threw the ball higher and higher. Every time it came down and she caught it. But this evening was different. As she neared a large pond on the edge of the woods, she threw the ball higher than before. With a loud Splaaash! the golden ball dropped into the water, out of sight.

"Oh dear!" the Princess wailed. She stood on the edge of the pond and looked carefully. But there was no sign of her lovely golden ball.

"Oh, what shall I do?" she cried, and began to sob bitterly.

"Whatever is the matter, why are you crying so, little Princess?" asked a kind voice behind her. "Your tears would melt the stones. What *is* the matter?"

The Princess gave a little hiccup and sobbed again. Then she saw a big, ugly green frog looking at her from the pond. "Oh, can you help me?" she begged. "My lovely golden ball has fallen into the pond and I shall never see it again." And she began to cry afresh.

"Is *that* all?" said the frog, looking at her. He seemed to be smiling, but he was so ugly she couldn't be sure.

"It's my special golden ball and I love it dearly," said the Princess sobbing still more. "And now I shall never see it again!"

"Oh do stop crying," said the frog. "Your golden ball is quite safe. I can get it whenever I like. But what will you give me if I do?"

"Anything, anything!" The Princess clapped her hands in delight. "Oh please hurry," and she jumped up and down. 'Hurry, hurry, and give me my ball. I'll give you clothes, jewels, even the golden crown I wear on special days! Only *please* get my golden ball for me!"

"Just a minute," said the frog. "What good would your clothes, your jewels, even the golden crown be to me? But if you can let me be your friend for three days, let me sit beside you at the table, eat from your little golden plate, drink from your little golden cup and, last of all, sleep in your bed—if you will promise me this, then I will get the golden ball for you."

"Oh yes, yes, dear kind frog," said the Princess, "I'll promise anything you say. Only please hurry and bring the golden ball to me!"

Now the Princess thought to herself that the silly old frog did not mean what he said. He could only live in the water and make a horrid croak. He could never be her playmate. Still, as long as he gave her back the golden ball it didn't matter about a promise. She must take care not to play by the pond again. And she held out her hand for the golden ball.

As soon as he heard her promise, the frog dived deep, deep down into the pond and soon emerged, the golden ball in his mouth. He jumped out of the water and dropped the ball at the feet of the Princess who picked it up, looked at it to see if it was hurt, then dried it off on the edge of her dress. "Oh my dearest little golden ball! How happy I am to have you back again." In her delight, she kissed the ball, and threw it up in the air, but not very high, for she did not want to lose it again. And laughing and singing she skipped away back to the palace, without giving the frog a word of thanks or a second thought.

"Wait for me," panted the frog. "I can't keep up with you." But the Princess was soon out of sight, her promise forgotten. As for the frog he climbed back into the pond again. That night when all the Court was at supper, the Princess was surprised to hear a voice calling her. There was a strange, splish, splash, sploshing sound at the door.

"Youngest Princess, let me in.

Open the door for me."

Everyone was very surprised. Quickly the Princess ran to the door, and there sat the frog, green , wet and cold. At once she shut the door in his face! The King, seeing she was afraid asked her, "What is the matter my child? What has frightened you?"

"Oh Father," she sobbed and he put his arms round her.

"Is it a giant come to take you away, my child?" he said. "Have no fear, I will send him away."

"Oh no, it's not a giant," sobbed the Princess, "it's a horrid, wet, green frog."

"Whatever does he want of you?" asked the King.

"Father, I was playing by the pond today and my golden ball fell into the water. The frog brought it back to me and I promised he could be my friend. But I never thought he would leave the pond. I never thought he would find me here. Now he is here and wants to eat from my plate, drink from my cup and," she gave a little wail, "sleep in my bed."

As she spoke, there was another knock at the door, and the frog called out again:

"Youngest Princess let me in.

Open the door for me."

"Oh send him away, please Father!" cried the Princess. "He's so ugly and horrid, I couldn't bear him near me!"

But the King looked at her sternly. "Daughter, when you make a promise you must keep it," he said. "Go and open the door."

The Princess hesitated but her father nodded, "Go on." So she went slowly to the door and opened it wide. The frog hopped in and followed her until he reached her chair. Then he sat close to her chair. "Please lift me up," he said.

The Princess thought him horrid, all cold and clammy, but one look from her father made her bend down and lift the frog on to her chair.

"Please put me on the table," said the frog, and she did so, trying not to look at him.

"If you push your plate closer, we can both eat from it," said the frog. Once again she obeyed him, but felt as if every mouthful would choke her. The frog ate all the food and then asked for a drink from her golden cup.

"I feel sleepy now," said the frog. "Please take me to your bedroom."

The Princess began to cry again. This was too much. She had let the horrid frog into the room, in front of all the Court. She had lifted him on to her chair and then the table, had shared her food and wine with him. This was more than she could bear!

"Please take me to your bed," said the frog again.

"It is only fair," said the King. "After all he helped you, it is only fair that you should help him now. Go on, take him up to your bed."

With a shudder, the Princess picked up the frog, holding him at arms' length and carried him to her room. There she dropped him on to the floor, as far away from her bed as she dared. Then she climbed into bed. What a horrid day she had had!

Plop, plop, plopperty plop! The frog was hopping across the room and now sat by her bed. "The floor is so hard," he said, "I am tired and want to sleep on your soft bed. Please lift me up."

So the Princess bent down and lifted him up, laying him on the pillow beside her. As daylight broke, the frog disappeared, but she did not see him go.

The next night he came back again and once again knocked on the door.

"Youngest Princess let me in.

Open the door for me."

And once again she had to open the door, lift the frog on to her chair and the table, and share her food and wine with him. And last of all carry him to her bed. This time she put him at the foot of the bed, but he soon hopped up to lie beside her on the pillow. In the morning he had gone.

The next night the frog came again and shared her supper and her bed. But when she woke up on the third morning, the Princess was astounded to see that though the frog had gone, as usual, in his place was a handsome prince, the most handsome she had ever seen standing by her bed!

"Don't be afraid," he said. "A wicked fairy changed me into a frog. She put a spell on me, so that I would be a frog until a princess came and rescued me from the pond. But she must eat, drink and sleep with me for three nights. Then the spell would be broken."

"Oh how happy I am!" cried the Princess, for she had never seen such a handsome prince in all her life.

In due time, they were married and lived happily ever after. And you may be sure the Princess never again broke a promise!

Rumpelstiltskin

Once upon a time there was a poor miller who had a beautiful daughter. One day, by chance, he was talking to the King. He wanted to make himself important so he said proudly, "My daughter is the most beautiful in the land. And, what's more, she can spin gold out of straw!" Then he had second thoughts. What had he said? But it was too late. He had made a stupid boast. Maybe the King would not notice.

But the King was greedy. "You say your daughter can spin gold out of straw?" he asked. "This I must see for myself. Bring the girl to the palace tomorrow and I will see what she can do."

So next day the poor girl was brought to the palace by her father. "But I can't spin at all," she cried. "Whatever shall I do?" No one listened, and the King ordered that the girl be shut in a small room that was filled with straw. A spindle stood in the corner.

"Now set to work," said the King. "Spin all this straw into gold. If, by morning, you have failed, you shall die." And he went out and locked the door.

The miller's daughter lay on the floor and sobbed. She could not spin at all. What could she do? There was no escape.

Then she heard a tiny click and the door opened. A little man stood in the doorway.

"Why are you crying?" he asked. "What troubles you so?"

"The King has told me to spin all this straw into gold," cried the girl. "I don't know how to do it!"

The little man laughed. "That's easy! What will you give me if I do it for you?"

The miller's daughter looked up at him. "My necklace," she said. "I'll give you this necklace, here!"

"Very well," said the little man putting the necklace in his pocket. He sat down at the spinning wheel and soon a whirring sound filled the room. Piece by piece, the straw disappeared and turned into bobbins of fine gold thread.

"Oh thank you, oh thank you!" cried the miller's daughter, clapping her hands in delight. And the little man disappeared.

Next morning when the King unlocked the door he was amazed to see the room full of bobbins of gold thread. He picked up one, then another. It was amazing! The miller had not lied after all. "Now may I go home?" asked the miller's daughter.

But the King shook his head. He was a greedy man and wanted more.

"No, you can stay here in the palace," he said. "Tonight you shall spin straw in an even bigger room." And the poor girl was taken to a huge room with straw right up to the rafters.

"Spin this into gold by morning, or you will die," said the King locking the door. And the poor girl lay down and cried and cried. This was impossible.

Once again she heard a tiny click and the little man stood in the doorway.

"Weeping again, I see," he said. "What is it this time?"

"All this straw has to be spun into gold thread," she wailed, "whatever shall I do! He will kill me in the morning."

"Have no fear," said the little man. "I will do it for you. But what will you give me if I help you?"

The miller's daughter looked all round her. What could she give him? He had had her necklace. Then she remembered, she had a small ring on her little finger. "Here, take this," she said offering it to the little man, who put it in his pocket.

Soon, the little man was sitting in front of the spinning wheel, and the clickety-clack, clickety-clack filled the room. The miller's daughter watched the pile of straw turn into gold, and soon the rhythm soothed her and she fell asleep. The little man spun on and on, until the straw had all turned into shiny golden bobbins of thread. Then he stood up, dusted himself off, tidily put the spinning wheel away and disappeared.

In the morning the greedy King's eyes glowed when he saw all the gold that had been spun in the night.

"I can hardly believe my eyes!" he cried looking all around him. "Now, I have one more task for you, my girl."

"Oh, no, you cannot want me to spin more!" she cried.

But the greedy King took her to an even bigger room. There was even more straw piled here, up and up to the rafters, and there was so much there was hardly room for the girl and the spinning wheel.

"If you spin all this into gold by sunrise, I will marry you," said the King who felt he had riches enough.

This time the girl was not so worried. She sat and waited for the click of the lock that would tell her the little man had come.

"Oh, there you are," she cried. "I hoped you would come!"

"More straw to spin, then," said the little man looking all around him. "My, this is a large room, that's for sure! What will you give me if I spin this for you?"

The poor miller's daughter looked around her again. She had given the little man her necklace, she had given him her ring. She had nothing left.

"Well, what will you give me if I help you?" asked the little man.

"I have nothing left," said the poor girl sadly.

"Well, that's that," said the little man, turning to leave her.

"Please, oh please don't go," begged the girl, now in tears. "Please help me. I will give you anything."

"Anything?" asked the little man.

"Yes, yes, anything," said the girl, "only please help me."

"Very well," said the little man, "if you promise to give me your first child, I will spin the straw for you."

"Anything, anything," promised the miller's daughter, and the little man began spinning. Long before morning the straw had turned into golden bobbins. The little man stood up, dusted off his clothes and put away the spindle. As soon as he put it down, the magic left it.

"Remember your promise," he said to the miller's daughter and once again he disappeared.

Early next morning, very early because he could not wait to see so much gold, the King arrived.

"Is it finished?" he asked opening the door.

"Yes, Your Majesty," said the girl, "all finished."

The King looked all round him. There was even more than he had hoped for.

"Now you shall become the Queen," he said, "and no more straw to spin!"

So the miller's daughter became Queen, and was very happy. As time passed she forgot her promise to the little man and all the straw he had spun for her. There was great rejoicing in all the land when in time she bore a son. By now, the Queen had forgotten her promise to the little man who had helped her. But he remembered.

Early one morning, when she was playing with her baby, he came to her and reminded her of her promise. He held out his arms to take the child, but the Queen clung to her son.

"Please don't take him," she begged. "He is so tiny. Please don't take him away from me."

"But you promised me your first child!" said the little man. "Long ago when I helped you to spin the straw into gold. Now I have come to claim the child."

"But I needed your help," said the Queen. "I had nothing else to offer, you had my ring and my necklace. What could I do?"

"A promise is a promise," said the little man.

But the Queen cried and pleaded, her tears falling on to her son who began to whimper.

"I will give you anything—anything you ask, only please don't take my son. You can have gold, silver, jewels, you can have anything you want if you leave him," said the Queen.

The little man looked at her and was moved to pity. "Very well," he said. "I will give you one more chance. If you can guess my name in three days' time, I will let you keep the child. If not, he is mine." And he disappeared.

The Queen smiled. She was sure she would soon discover the name of the little man and keep her son.

She clapped her hands and messengers came from all over the palace.

"Bring me all the books you can find giving lists of boys' names!" she ordered. 'Tell me all the names you can think of!" And she sat up all night looking at first one name and then another. Which could it be? There were so many to choose from.

Next morning the little man suddenly appeared beside her. The Queen picked up the list of names she had written down.

"Is your name Albert, Cuthbert, William?" she asked.

"No," said the little man.

"Well, is it James, Timothy or Roderick?" she wondered.

"No," was the reply.

And so on, all the way down the list. The little man said every one of them was wrong, and he laughed and danced.

"You will never guess my name," he said and was gone.

It was the same the next day. Though the Queen and all the court had looked at hundreds and hundreds of names, the little man still shook his head at every name she suggested.

"But you must be Longlegs, or Sleepyhead or Little Ears?" she said desperately. She had tried to think of all the most unusual names in the world. But all were wrong.

"Ha, ha, he, he!" laughed the little man, "you will never guess my name in a hundred years!" And then he was gone.

The poor Queen was getting desperate. She only had one more day to guess the little man's name. Somehow, she must, she had to find out. She sent messengers all over the land, she made lists of all the names that the children were called, and had a list that stretched across the banqueting hall. But she was very sad, for she knew in her heart that none of them was the right one.

Very late that night one of her messengers returned. His clothes were torn and dusty for he had ridden many miles.

"What is it?" the Queen asked wearily. "Have you brought more names for my list?"

"Your Majesty," said the man, kneeling before her, "I have not found any new names, and this may be all rubbish, but I have heard something very strange!"

"Tell me, tell me," said the Queen, "anything might help."

"As I rode over the mountain," the messenger said, "I came to the edge of the wood, where the fox says goodnight to the hare."

"Yes, yes," interrupted the Queen, "go on!"

"Well, I saw a little clearing. Dancing round a fire and chanting a strange song, was a little man. I crept closer and this is what he said, it was a strange song!"

"Oh tell me the words," the Queen said urgently.

"It was something like this," said the messenger,

"Today I brew, tomorrow I bake,
The next day I the Queen's child take.
Little does she guess, the poor dame,
That Rumpelstiltskin is my name!"

41

"Rumpelstiltskin?" said the Queen. "That's a strange name!"

"Yes, that's what he said, Rumpelstiltskin," the messenger told her.

When she heard it the Queen was sure her messenger had found the right name. Her child was saved. She gave the man a bag of gold coins.

Next morning she was waiting when the little man appeared.

"Is your name Tom?" she asked.

"No, no," he cried, dancing with glee.

"Is it Henry, then?" said the Queen, teasing a little.

"No, no, no," said the little man. "One more guess and the child is mine!" And he jumped up and down.

"Well, then," said the Queen, "I know! It must be Rumpelstiltskin!"

The little man gave a scream of rage.

"Who told you? Who told you? It's witchcraft! It's magic!" and he screamed and raged. "Rumpelstiltskin *is* my name!"

The little man was so angry, he jumped and stamped his feet so hard he disappeared through the floor, and no one ever saw him again.

So the Queen kept her son, and lived very happily.

The Hare and the Hedgehog

When I was very young, my grandfather used to tell me this story:

"It isn't true! It's all lies," I would say every time. And he would always reply, "But if it is not true, no one would tell it to you!"

This is the story he told me.

It was a fine, sunny morning, and Hedgehog was very happy. He hummed as he stood at his door. Mrs Hedgehog was getting his breakfast, and he could smell the cooking.

"Is breakfast ready yet?" he called out to his wife.

"Give me another ten minutes!" she called back, "you know you like it crispy."

So Hedgehog decided to go for a walk. He strolled along watching the bees buzzing round the flowers. "I know, I'll go and see how my turnips are doing," he said to himself and walked over to the patch.

The turnips grew in a corner of a big field. The farmer owned the field, but he didn't mind the hedgehogs having some of the fine turnips that grew there. So Hedgehog always said it was *his* turnip patch!

Halfway across the field, Hedgehog met Hare who was looking at the cabbages. They, too, belonged to the farmer, but Hare liked to eat them, and he boasted they were *his* cabbages.

"Good morning, Hare," said Hedgehog as he passed.

But Hare, who imagined he was a very fine fellow, did not bother to reply. He looked at the hedgehog, up and down, up and down, and then he said scornfully, "I wonder how you get up so early with your short legs!"

This made Hedgehog cross because he hated anyone to talk about his little legs.

"What's wrong with my legs?" he asked, "they're very good legs!"

"Good legs, huh! laughed Hare, "just look at them! All short and fat and," and he pointed, "*crooked*!" And he shook with laughter.

"So you think my legs are crooked, do you?" snapped Hedgehog in

44

a rage. "I can walk as well with them as you. I can even run with them. Faster than you! So there!" And he drew himself up and frowned at the hare who was still shaking with mirth.

"Oh, that's good," said Hare, "you say you can run with those legs. That's something I'd like to see! Run with those legs, those crooked, bent legs," and he went on laughing and pointing at the little hedgehog.

"If you care to have a race, I'll win!" said Hedgehog. "Well, what do you say?"

"A race?" scoffed Hare, "but it would be no contest. You can't run at all!"

"What do you want for a prize then?" asked the hedgehog, ignoring his rudeness. "How about a gold coin, and the loser to give a party for all the other animals?"

"Oh, it's too silly, but, all right, let's race," said the hare. "If that's what you want. I don't mind having a gold coin, any day. And you had better start getting ready for the party."

"Don't be too sure," said Hedgehog. "When shall we race? How about tomorrow?"

"Any day's fine with me. Tomorrow will do as well as any other," said the hare, "about ten?"

"Agreed," said the hedgehog, and hurried home as fast as his legs would carry him.

All the way home, Hedgehog made his plans. He *would* outwit that horrid Hare!

"Wife, Wife!" he called as he ran up the path, "come quickly!"

"Whatever is the matter?" she asked, drying her paws on her apron. "Breakfast is all ready."

"No time for that," he said briskly. "We have to make plans. I have just told Hare I can beat him in a race. Tomorrow! The prize is a gold coin and a party for all the other animals."

"You said what!" exclaimed his wife. She could not believe he was so silly.

"Just listen to me," he told her. "I need your help for my plan."

So, forgetting all about his breakfast, Hedgehog took his wife and showed her the field where they would race next day.

"See here," he said, "Hare will run in one furrow, and I will run in another. We will start at the top and finish by the big tree. But the secret is this, we'll dress alike and *you* will wait at the end, so, when Hare is coming, you can jump out and run over the line. So you will win the race."

"What a good idea!" she said. "Now come and have your meal."

Next day the sun shone, and all the animals gathered to watch the race. They were all talking and wondering how the hedgehog would beat the hare. They all *hoped* he would, but either way they would have a party. It was all very exciting!

Hare was stretching his long legs, jumping up and down. He was full of bounce.

"Where's that hedgehog then?" he called. "Chickened out, hasn't he? No wonder!"

"I'm here, and ready," said Hedgehog quietly from the furrow. Fox was the starter, and both animals stood in line at the top of the field. As soon as the fox shouted, "Go!" Hare bounded away and was soon out of sight. Hedgehog ran a few steps then hid in the furrow and waited. Hare ran on, his long ears flapping in the wind. He was doing well, but as he came almost to the end, he heard a voice say, "I've won, I'm here!" All the animals clapped their paws and cheered. He could not believe it! But there, at the end was the hedgehog, smiling and so pleased with himself! Hedgehog beaten Hare! There must be a mistake, the hedgehog had not passed him. Panting, Hare cried, "Let's do it again, from this end!"

"All right," said Hedgehog, and once more the fox started them off.

This time Hare ran so fast his feet scarcely touched the ground. But once again, he heard Hedgehog say, "I'm here, I've won." And there he was at the finish!

So all the morning, they ran their race, backwards and forwards, until the hare was gasping for breath. The little hedgehog was fresh and cool. How *did* he do it?

"All right," gasped Hare," you win. I can't run any more. Here is the coin! As soon as I can breathe again, I'll get the party ready."

So all the animals cheered and patted the little hedgehog on the head and said he was a fine fellow. And the party was the best they had ever had. Sitting by his fire at night, Hare often wonders how he was beaten, but Hedgehog will never tell him. He had the gold coin framed and put over his fireplace for all to see.